EL DORADO

Lights! Action! California!

Sacramento

Arnold

Son

SAN
JOAQUIN

Reader's Digest Young Families

Senior Designer: Elaine Lopez
Editor: Sharon Fass Yates
Editorial Director: Pamela Pia

Published by Reader's Digest Young Families, an imprint of The Reader's Digest Association, Inc.
Reader's Digest Road, Pleasantville, NY U.S.A. 10570-7000
Written by Christina Wilsdon copyright © 2006 Reader's Digest Young Families.
Illustrations by Dennis Hockerman copyright © 2006 Reader's Digest Young Families.
Page 27: California Quail copyright © 1982 Reader's Digest Association, Inc. California map and Golden Poppy
copyright © 1992 Reader's Digest Association, Inc. Background map copyright © 2005 Map Resources.

Library of Congress Cataloging-in-Publication Data

Wilsdon, Christina.
   Lights! Action! California! / written by Christina Wilsdon ; illustrated
by Dennis Hockerman.
     p. cm. -- (Read and write with the country mouse and the city
mouse)
   Summary: While visiting California, Henry the city mouse and Emma
the country mouse get to star in a movie that is being shot in Hollywood,
San Francisco, and among giant redwood trees.
   ISBN-13: 978-1-59939-009-3
   ISBN-10: 1-59939-009-4
     (1. Motion pictures--Production and direction--Fiction. 2.Mice--Fiction.
3. Animals--Fiction. 4. California--Fiction.)   I. Hockerman, Dennis, ill.
II. Title. III. Series: Wilsdon, Christina. Read and write with the country
mouse and the city mouse.
PZ7.W68577Llg 2006
(E)--dc22
                                          2005035095

Printed in China.
10 9 8 7 6 5 4 3 2 1

Read and Write with
The Country Mouse and the City Mouse

Lights! Action! California!

Written by
Christina Wilsdon

Illustrated by
Dennis Hockerman

Reader's Digest Young Families

"Ah, California. This is the life!" said Henry as he gazed out at the Pacific Ocean. "Breathe in that sea air!"

His cousin Emma sniffed. "It *is* great," she said, "but what is that other wonderful smell? It's making me hungry!"

"Tacos," said Henry, pointing to a taco stand nearby. "Another big-city treat for you, my dear country cousin!"

"Extra cheese on mine, please!" cried Emma as Henry trotted over to the stand.

After lunch, Emma and Henry dipped their toes in the surf.
"The water's great!" said Emma. "Let's go—"
Thump! A surfboard suddenly scooted in between Henry and
Emma, closely followed by a very wet mouse.
"Whew! That wave dumped me at the last second!" the mouse
said laughing.
"Surfing looks like fun," said Henry. "Is it hard to do?"
"Want to give it a try?" asked the mouse. "I'll teach you."
"Yes, indeed!" cried Henry.

Emma clapped as Henry balanced on the surfboard and glided across the ocean. A big wave curled under him and lifted him high.

"He's a natural!" said a chipmunk, standing behind Emma.

"He's my cousin," said Emma proudly.

"My name's Chip," said the chipmunk. "I'm a movie director. My crew and I are looking for new actors. How would you and your cousin like to be movie stars for a few days?"

"Movie stars?" Emma squealed. "Whee! Just wait until I tell my country friends!"

"It's a spy movie," Chip explained to Emma and Henry. "You two will play the heroes. You must bring a very important message to the chief spy, whose name is Big Cheese. You will be chased by Sasha here. She is playing the role of the evil Captain Cat."

Henry and Emma looked nervously at Sasha—a Siamese cat! "Don't worry," purred Sasha slyly. "I only eat sushi!"

In no time at all, Henry and Emma were in costume and ready to go. Cameras rolled. "Action!" shouted Chip.

Henry and Emma's first job was to jump into a car and dash away. They had to do this over and over again until Chip said, "That's a wrap!"

Bright and early the next morning, Henry and Emma were back in costume.

"I'm not used to being up at this hour!" said Henry, yawning.

"Oh, I'm always up with the birds," said Emma. "In the country, we get up early to start our chores."

"You're going to be up with the birds all day today!" said Chip, laughing. "The next scene takes place way up there!"

He pointed to the top of a big set of letters perched on a hillside above them.

"HOLLYWOOD," read Emma.

"The movie-making capital of the world!" bragged Chip.

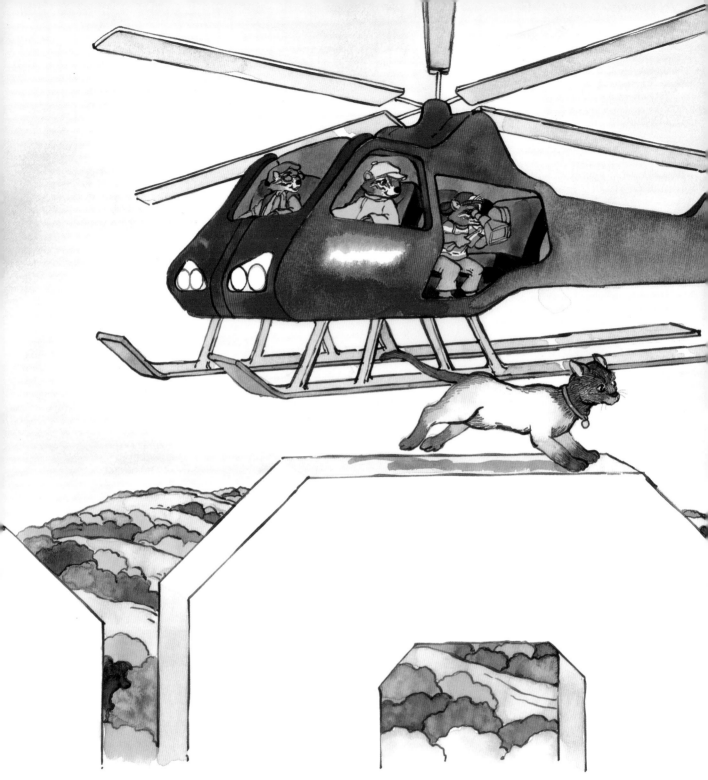

"Wow!" said Emma after arriving on top of the letter H. "You can see for miles!"

"Your job today is to run away from Sasha. Then you will be rescued by Cal. He's a California condor. Places, everyone!" shouted Chip.

Henry and Emma looked up to see a huge bird soaring in the sky.

On cue, Sasha chased Henry and Emma from the letter H all the way to the letter D at the end of the word. Just as they reached the edge, the condor swooped down and rescued the mice cousins.

"Next stop is the city of San Francisco!" said the condor, flapping his mighty wings. "That's where the next scene of the film takes place."

Fog swirled above Henry and Emma the next morning as they trudged up one of San Francisco's steep hills.

"How marvelous to be in a city," said Henry, sighing happily. "And what a marvelous city to be in!"

"I can't see the city because of the fog," said Emma.

Ding-ding! A cable car pulled up beside them.

"Hop aboard!" shouted Chip. "This is the best way to go uphill in San Francisco!"

All morning, Henry and Emma hopped on and off cable cars as
Sasha chased after them. They stopped filming at lunchtime.

"I'm tuckered out," said Emma.

"Phew," said Henry. "As a city mouse, I thought I was used to a fast pace. But I'm worn out, too!"

"Let's take a break," said Chip. "Do you want to go to Chinatown for some chop suey?"

"There's a town inside the city?" squeaked Emma. "Goodness me!"

The next day, Chip took Henry and Emma to see the Golden Gate Bridge.

Emma looked at the bridge with surprise. "I thought it would be a gold color," she said. "Why is it orange?"

"So ships can see it better," explained Henry.

"Today we will film you escaping across the bridge," said Chip. "You'll make your getaway while Sasha gets stuck in traffic."

"Henry, will you take a picture of me with the bridge?" asked Emma. "We've been so busy, we've hardly taken any pictures at all—except for the ones in the movie!"

"Certainly," said Henry. He held up the camera. "Say cheese!"

"The next scene takes place in Redwood National Park," said Chip as they drove north on the highway. "Home of the tallest trees in the world!"

"All trees are tall," said Emma, "if you're a mouse!"

When they arrived in the park, Emma saw what Chip meant!
The redwood trees seemed to reach up to the clouds.
   "I've visited lots of cities," said Henry, "but these trees are taller
than lots of skyscrapers I've seen!"

"We'll shoot the final scene today," said Chip. "The one in which you deliver the message to Big Cheese at the top of a tree."

Henry and Emma looked at each other nervously.

"Do we have to climb all the way up there?" asked Emma, pointing.

"No," said Chip. "We're going to use a little movie-making magic!"

Chip showed them a giant redwood lying on the forest floor. "Just creep along the side of this tree and pretend you're climbing," he said. "In the movie, it will look as if you are climbing up instead of sideways!"

The movie's last scene took place at the top of the tree.

"Here you go," said Henry as he gave a slip of paper to Big Cheese.

Sasha came to a screeching halt behind Henry and Emma. "Rats! Foiled again!" said Sasha.

"At last!" cried Big Cheese. "Thanks to you two, we finally have the secret code. Now we can open the Mouse Trap and free all the brave mice captured by the evil Captain Cat!"

"Cut!" shouted Chip. "Excellent job, everybody! That's a wrap!"

"Well, that was a lot fun," said Emma. "But I think I'm ready to go back to the peace and quiet of the countryside. Show biz is too busy for me!"

"Let's go take that dip in the ocean first," suggested Henry.

A few weeks later, Emma and Henry settled into red velvet seats
in an old movie theater.

"The first screening of our movie," said Emma. "How exciting!
What did Chip end up calling it?"

"It's called *The Big Cheese*," said Henry. "*Shh*, it's starting!"

And so they settled back to watch the movie, munching their
popcorn happily.